Teachers, librarians, and kids from across Canada are talking about the *Canadian Flyer Adventures*. Here's what some of them had to say:

Great Canadian historical content, excellent illustrations, and superb closing historical facts (I love the kids' commentary!). ~ *SARA S., TEACHER, ONTARIO*

As a teacher–librarian I welcome this series with open arms. It fills the gap for Canadian historical adventures at an early reading level! There's fast action, interesting, believable characters, and great historical information. ~ *MARGARET L., TEACHER–LIBRARIAN, BRITISH COLUMBIA*

The *Canadian Flyer Adventures* will transport young readers to different eras of our past with their appealing topics. Thank goodness there are more artifacts in that old dresser ... they are sure to lead to even more escapades. ~ *SALLY B., TEACHER–LIBRARIAN, MANITOBA*

When I shared the book with a grade 1–2 teacher at my school, she enjoyed the book, noting that her students would find it appealing because of the action-adventure and short chapters. ~ *HEATHER J., TEACHER AND LIBRARIAN, NOVA SCOTIA*

Newly independent readers will fly through each *Canadian Flyer Adventure*, and be asking for the next installment! Children will enjoy the fast-paced narrative, the personalities of the main characters, and the drama of the dangerous situations the children find themselves in. ~ *PAM L., LIBRARIAN, ONTARIO*

I love the fact that these are Canadian adventures—kids should know how exciting Canadian history is. Emily and Matt are regular kids, full of curiosity, and I can see readers relating to them. ~ *JEAN K., TEACHER, ONTARIO*

What kids told us:

I would like to have the chance to ride on a magical sled and have adventures. ~ *EMMANUEL*

I would like to tell the author that her book is amazing, incredible, awesome, and a million times better than any book I've read. ~ *MARIA*

I would recommend the *Canadian Flyer Adventures* series to other kids so they could learn about Canada too. The book is just the right length and hard to put down. ~ *PAUL*

The books I usually read are the full-of-fact encyclopedias. This book is full of interesting ideas that simply grab me. ~ *ELEANOR*

At the end of the book Matt and Emily say they are going on another adventure. I'm very interested in where they are going next! ~ *ALEX*

I like when Emily and Matt fly into the sky on a sled towards a new adventure. I can't wait for the next book! ~ *JI SANG*

All Aboard!

Frieda Wishinsky

Illustrated by Leanne Franson

MAPLE
TREE
PRESS

Maple Tree Press books are published by Owlkids Books Inc.
10 Lower Spadina Avenue, Suite 400, Toronto, Ontario M5V 2Z2
www.mapletreepress.com

Text © 2008 Frieda Wishinsky   Illustrations © 2008 Leanne Franson

Distributed in Canada by Raincoast Books
9050 Shaughnessy Street, Vancouver, British Columbia V6P 6E5

Distributed in the United States by Publishers Group West
1700 Fourth Street, Berkeley, California 94710

Dedication
For my friend Norah McClintok

Acknowledgements
Many thanks to the hard-working Maple Tree team—Sheba Meland, Anne Shone, Grenfell
Featherstone, Deborah Bjorgan, Cali Hoffman, Dawn Todd, and Erin Walker—for their insightful
comments and steadfast support. Special thanks to Leanne Franson and Claudia Dávila for their
engaging and energetic illustrations and design.

Cataloguing in Publication Data
Wishinsky, Frieda
All aboard! / Frieda Wishinsky ; illustrated by Leanne Franson.

(Canadian flyer adventures ; 9)
ISBN 978-1-897349-38-0 (bound). ISBN 978-1-897349-39-7 (pbk.)

1. Canadian Pacific Railway Company—History—Juvenile fiction.
2. Railroads—Canada—History—Juvenile fiction.
I. Franson, Leanne II. Title. III. Series.

PS8595.I834A64 2008   jC813'.54   C2008-902038-3

Library of Congress Control Number: 2008925708

Design & art direction: Claudia Dávila
Illustrations: Leanne Franson

We acknowledge the financial support of the Canada Council
for the Arts, the Ontario Arts Council, the Government
of Canada through the Book Publishing Industry Development Program (BPIDP), and the
Government of Ontario through the Ontario Media Development Corporation's Book Initiative
for our publishing activities.

ONTARIO ARTS COUNCIL
CONSEIL DES ARTS DE L'ONTARIO

Printed in Canada
Ancient Forest Friendly: Printed on 100% Post-Consumer Recycled Paper

A   B   C   D   E   F

CONTENTS

HOW IT ALL BEGAN

Emily and Matt couldn't believe their luck. They discovered an old dresser full of strange objects in the tower of Emily's house. They also found a note from Emily's Great-Aunt Miranda: "The sled is yours. Fly it to wonderful adventures."

They found a sled right behind the dresser! When they sat on it, shimmery gold words appeared:

*Rub the leaf
Three times fast.
Soon you'll fly
To the past.*

The sled rose over Emily's house. It flew over their town of Glenwood. It sailed out of a cloud and into the past. Their adventures on the flying sled had begun! Where will the sled take them next? Turn the page to find out.

1

Old Train

"Guess what!" said Matt, racing up Emily's front steps. "I just saw a model of an awesome old train at school."

Emily laughed. "You and your trains. All you think about is trains."

"And dinosaurs. And pirates. I think about other stuff, too," Matt protested. "But I love trains, especially old ones. Let's go to the tower and see if the magic sled will take us on a train adventure."

"Well…," said Emily, rolling her eyes.

"Come on, Em! I really want to go."

Emily grinned. "Okay. Why not?" She popped her sketchbook into her pocket. "I'll draw a picture of the train zooming down the track. Do you have your recorder with you?"

Matt patted his pocket. "Yes, and I'll record all the old train chugging sounds."

Emily and Matt hurried up the rickety stairs to the tower room.

Inside, Emily opened the bottom drawer of the mahogany dresser. "I've never checked this drawer before."

The friends peered inside. There was a handkerchief, an old stuffed bear, and a whistle. "No train stuff here," said Emily.

"Wait," said Matt, pointing to the metal whistle in a corner. "Conductors on old trains blew whistles, didn't they? Maybe this is an old train whistle. What does the label say?"

Emily read it out aloud. "Train to Last Spike, Craigellachie, B.C., 1885."

"Yahoo! It *is* an old train whistle. And B.C. stands for British Columbia. They have lots of mountains there. Imagine riding a train through a high mountain pass."

Emily's eyes lit up. "That would be great. But what's the last spike?"

"A spike is like a big nail. They use it on rail tracks. But I don't know why this one was the last."

"Let's find out," said Emily, pulling the Canadian Flyer out from behind the dresser.

"All aboard," sang Matt as he and Emily hopped on.

As soon as they were seated, shimmery gold words appeared on the front of the sled.

Rub the leaf
Three times fast.
Soon you'll fly
To the past.

Matt rubbed the leaf, and immediately fog enveloped the sled. It rose over Emily's house, over Glenwood, and into a fluffy white cloud.

When the sled burst out of the cloud, it headed down.

"I don't see a train. I don't see anything," said Emily. "And it's dark and cold out. I can feel snow. Where are we going?"

" I... I...have no idea," said Matt through chattering teeth. "But we're going down fast.

Emily pointed to a freight train speeding down the track. "Oh no! We're heading for the top of *that*. What kind of train adventure is this?"

2

Rattle and Roll

The sled landed hard on a pile of rails stacked on the freight train's flatcar.

A boy was curled up on the steel rails. He rubbed his eyes and stared at them. He looked about seventeen. His jacket, pants, and shirt were rumpled and grimy. His hat was half off his head.

"Where did you two come from?" he muttered.

"We came from...from...," stammered Matt.

"From up there," Emily blurted out.

The boy sat up. "You mean you came over the pass on the train like I did?" he said. "But I didn't see you climb on the flatcar. I must have fallen asleep for a few minutes. I'm so tired and cold I can't see straight."

Emily shivered. "I'm so cold my toes feel like snowballs," she said.

"Yeah. We wanted to ride *inside* a train," said Matt. "Not freeze on top of one."

"I know. Who wants to be rattled and rolled on an open flatcar?" grunted the boy. "But it's the only way we're going to see the Last Spike ceremony."

Emily and Matt glanced at each other—so the last spike was some kind of ceremony.

"And it's the only way I'm going to find my buddy, Alex," the boy continued. "I haven't heard from him in two months."

The boy looked down. "I hope Alex isn't one

of the railroad workers who's been injured…or worse."

"I hope your friend is okay," said Emily. "Will there be lots of people at the Last Spike ceremony?"

"All the railroad big shots like Mr. William Van Horne, Mr. Donald Smith, and Mr. Sanford Fleming will be there. It's an important day. Canada will finally be linked by rail. I can't wait to see them hammer in that last spike. And I can't wait to see Alex. My name's Edward Mallandaine, by the way."

"I'm Matt. And this is Emily."

Edward stared at Emily. "You're a girl? You're wearing overalls like a boy."

Emily looked down at her clothes. She was wearing blue overalls and a rough brown jacket. Her ponytail was tucked into a cap. Matt was wearing a similar outfit.

"It's easier to travel in these clothes," she explained.

"You're not kidding," said Edward. "It wouldn't be fun sitting on a dirty flatcar in a dress. And you were smart to bring your sled. If the snow sticks, at least one of you can ride around when we get off the train."

"Do you think we'll be there soon?" asked Emily.

"Craigellachie is not far from here. We'll get there while it's still dark. I don't know about you, but I plan to find a place to sleep till the ceremony begins. I'm so tired that if I don't sleep, I'm going to walk smack into a tree. I..."

Before Edward could finish his sentence, the flatcar hit a bump. Emily and Matt tumbled forward and smashed into Edward.

"Sorry," said Emily.

"Are you hurt?" asked Matt.

Edward pulled himself up. "Not much. Anyway what's another bump when you've been shook up all night like a pair of dice."

"Hey! The train's slowing down," said Matt.

"Finally!" said Edward.

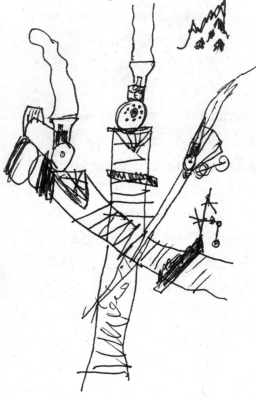

3

In the Dark

The train ground to a halt. Edward, Matt, and Emily stood up.

"Why don't I hop down first and you can pass me your sled," suggested Edward.

Edward held on to the side of the flatcar and climbed off. Matt and Emily picked up the sled. They hoisted it over the side by the rope. Edward grabbed it and pulled the sled to the ground.

"Now you two!" he called.

"It's farther down than I thought," said

nobrute!

Emily peering over the top of the flatcar.

"Come on. You can do it," said Edward. "You made it this far, and you're not wearing a dress!"

Emily sighed. "Okay. Here goes!" She held on to the side of the flatcar and edged herself down. As she neared the ground, her pants caught on a nail.

"I'm going to have a hole in my pants," she groaned.

"Don't worry about the hole. You've almost made it," said Edward.

Emily slid to the ground. "Yahoo!" she exclaimed. Then she leaned over and inspected her pants. "And my pants only have a little hole in them."

"My turn," said Matt. Matt slid down from the flatcar. Soon he was on the ground beside Emily and Edward.

The three children peered around. The snow had stopped and the moon peeked out from the clouds. But all they could see were trees, broken railway ties, and a boxcar sitting on the side of the tracks.

"I don't know about you, but I have to find a place to sleep," said Edward. "But where? There's not much around here, and it's pretty dark. I'd probably get lost if I walked around looking for a place."

"Maybe you could sleep inside that boxcar. At least it isn't moving, and it might be warmer inside than out," said Emily.

"It can't be any worse than that horrible flatcar," said Edward. "Are you two going to get some sleep?"

"I'm not tired," said Emily.

"Me neither," said Matt.

"Well, if you don't sleep, wake me when the

sun comes up. I want to find my friend Alex before the ceremony starts," said Edward.

Edward climbed up on a wooden step at the side of the boxcar. Then he slid the door open. He waved and popped inside.

Emily and Matt sat on the sled. "Now what do we do?" asked Emily.

"It's too dark to explore. We'll have to wait for the sun to rise."

Emily wrapped her arms around herself. "It's so cold here. Maybe we should go inside that boxcar and stay warm."

Matt grimaced. "I'd rather stay outside. It looks creepy in that boxcar. There might be mice or rats crawling around."

"If there were, Edward wouldn't stay there."

Matt laughed. "I think Edward is so tired, he wouldn't notice if a rat sat on his head!"

"You're right," said Emily. "Let's stay outside. But the sun better come up soon. I don't like sitting out here. It's cold and quiet. It's like no one's around except us."

"Listen. There is something—or someone—else around," said Matt. "Can you hear those crunching sounds?"

15

4

What's that Noise?

"I hear it too," said Emily. "But I can't see anything. What's making the noise?"

"Is there anybody out there?" called Matt.

No one answered.

"There goes that noise again," said Matt. "What if it's a bear? There are lots of bears in British Columbia."

Emily gulped. "Don't they hibernate by now?" she asked.

"Sometimes they do, but sometimes they don't till later."

"The sound is coming from behind us," said Emily.

"Okay. Let's get off the sled, very, very slowly," said Matt. "You don't want the bear to think you're scared."

"It might not be a bear," said Emily.

"Let's turn around and see," said Matt. "If it is a bear, you shouldn't turn your back to it."

"I'm glad you know so much about bears," said Emily turning slowly. "If there's one behind us, I'll probably scream."

"You can't do that," said Matt.

And then they saw it.

Emily laughed. "Yahoo! It's not a bear. It's a little deer."

The deer stared at them. Then it sniffed the air and scurried back into the woods.

"I guess we scared it," said Emily. "I'm glad it wasn't a bear."

"It could have been a bear," said Matt. "And we still might see one around here."

Emily patted Matt on the shoulder. "Don't worry so much, Matt. Soon lots of people will be arriving for the Last Spike ceremony, and bears aren't invited. Hey, I can hear people's voices, now. Can you?"

Matt and Emily peered around. "Where are they? It sounds like someone's hammering metal. Maybe they're putting down rails," said Matt.

"And look! The sun is beginning to rise. Let's wake Edward and see what's going on!" said Emily.

Emily and Matt raced back to the boxcar. They scrambled up the wooden step and knocked on the door.

"Wake up, Edward. The sun's coming up!" called Matt.

"Go away," mumbled Edward. "I just fell asleep. It can't be time to get up already."

"It's time," said Emily. "We hear people and banging. We want to see what's going on."

"Okay. Okay. I'm coming."

In a few seconds, Edward's head peeked out through the boxcar door. He squinted, and then he smiled. "So, what are we waiting for?" He hopped off the boxcar.

"Which way?" asked Matt.

"The sound is coming from back along the track," said Edward.

"I think it's coming from ahead," said Emily.

"Why don't we first go back along the track, and if nothing's happening that way, we can turn around," suggested Matt.

"Okay," said Emily. "I'm just glad we're going to find people and not bears."

5

Don't Move

They walked back along the track. They could still hear banging, but not as loudly as before.

"I think we should walk the other way," said Emily. "I'm sure the banging is coming from there."

"No. I'm sure it's this way," Edward insisted. "Come on. Let's go a little farther."

They took another step, and then suddenly Edward signalled them to stop. "Don't move," he said between clenched teeth.

"Why not?" asked Emily.

"There's a black bear up there." Edward pointed to a thickly wooded area not far from the tracks.

The children froze. They stared as a big black bear lumbered down the hill. It clambered onto the tracks and picked up something, stuck it into its mouth, and chomped.

"It's found some food," said Edward. "Maybe it will eat and go away."

"I don't think so," said Emily. "There's more food closer to us." Emily pointed to the tracks beside them, where someone had left a pile of apple peels and hardened bread crusts.

"Oh no," said Edward. "We're in trouble now."

"We have to make noise and walk slowly away, but we can't turn our backs on the bear. And we can't look straight in its eyes," said Matt.

Edward gulped. "You're right." He yelled

and clapped his hands as he inched back.

Emily and Matt shouted and clapped their hands, too. They took careful, slow steps back.

The bear looked up at them. It scurried toward the pile of peels and old bread.

"Make more noise. Make louder noise!" shouted Edward.

The children yelled and clapped, but still the bear kept coming.

"W...what now?" said Emily. "My knees are so wobbly I don't know if I can walk."

"You can. You have to. Keep walking and keep making noise. Throw something," said Edward.

Matt picked up a handful of rocks and threw it in the bear's direction. Emily and Edward picked up rocks and threw them, too.

But the bear still kept coming. It reached the pile of food and bent over to eat.

"Don't panic," said Edward, swallowing hard. "Maybe it will eat the food and go away."

The children kept walking backwards and shouting, but the bear wouldn't budge.

"It's not leaving," said Emily. "Yikes. It's coming towards us again!"

The bear gobbled down the last bit of food and roared. Then it headed toward the children.

"Keep moving," said Edward in a shaky voice.

"I'm so scared I think my heart is going to jump into my throat," said Matt.

"My heart's already in my throat," said Edward.

The bear roared again. Then it stopped and looked up the hill. Two big cubs stood at the top.

The bear on the tracks roared louder. It scurried up the hill like a rabbit. In an instant all three bears raced into the thick woods.

"That was close," said Emily.

"Let's get out of here before the bears come back," said Edward.

6

Drippy Adventure

"You were right, Emily," said Edward. "We need to turn right. Let's find people before we meet any more bears."

The three friends ran to the right. The ground was slick with melting snow and mud. They stumbled on rocks and sank into mud up to their ankles.

Matt picked up the sled. "I'd better carry it. It's getting messed up."

"So am I!" said Edward. "This mud is as thick as soup. My shoes and pants are soaked."

Matt and Emily looked down at their pants. Their pants and shoes were wet and caked with mud, too.

"This is one drippy adventure," Emily whispered to Matt as they hurried toward the voices.

"I know, and we haven't even had a ride on a real train yet."

"But there goes that banging again," said Emily. "I think we're close to people."

The children ran on. The banging grew louder and louder.

"There's the engine that pulled us!" cried Matt. "It looks as big and black as I imagined."

"Over there!" shouted Emily. They crossed in front of the engine to the main tracks, where a group of railroad workers were bent over, hammering down rails.

The children raced toward them.

"Good morning," said Edward, huffing and out of breath. "I'm Edward, and this is Emily and Matt. We're here to see the ceremony for the last spike. Do you—"

"I have no time to talk to children," grunted a railroad worker. He was as skinny as the rails he was pounding. He waved them away with his hand.

"Don't mind Lou. We've all been working in the snow and mud to finish this railroad. We're sick and tired," said a burly, bearded man. "My name's Henry."

Henry stuck a dirt-smeared hand out to Edward.

"Good to meet you," said Edward, shaking Henry's hand. "Do you know my friend Alex Smith? He's a railroad worker. He was working around here."

Henry scratched his beard. "I don't know

anyone called Alex. I've just been here a week. Ask the fellows over there." Henry pointed to three men sitting on a log and munching on bread.

Edward, Matt, and Emily ran over to the three men on the log. "Do you know a railroad worker named Alex?" asked Edward.

"I know an Alex," said the shortest of the three men. "He was in a bad accident. I don't know what happened to him."

Edward's face fell. "You...you don't think he's dead, do you?" he stammered.

"I don't know. I heard he was pinned under a falling tree. His friends carried him away. I haven't heard anything since. We've been too busy finishing this railroad to check on anyone. Don't worry, kid. He might be alive."

Edward swallowed hard. Emily and Matt could tell he was trying not to cry.

"Alex is my best buddy," said Edward. "I have to see him again. Do you think anyone would know what happened to him or where he is?"

"Ask Sanford Fleming," said one of the other men. "Alex helped him survey. He might know what happened. Mr. Fleming is arriving on the railroad with all the officials this morning."

7

The Last Spike

"Ladies and gentlemen," said Matt into his recorder, "the special train carrying the builders of the Canadian Pacific Railway is rumbling toward us, on the main track. It's belching thick, black smoke. It's cold and foggy outside, but any moment now the men who made the railway possible will be here to celebrate the Last Spike."

"Hurry! Turn that off," said Emily. "Here comes Edward."

Matt snapped his recorder off.

Just then Edward came running toward them.

"Here," he said, handing them each a chunk of dark bread. "You must be as hungry as I am. The railway workers gave this to me."

"Thanks," said Emily. She stared at the bread. It was as hard as a rock. "I don't really like bread without butter and jam," she told Edward.

"And I'm not that hungry," said Matt.

"I'll have it if you won't," said Edward. "I'm starving."

Edward bit into the bread.

"Look! Here's the train!" said Matt. "It looks and sounds just the way I imagined."

As the train rattled down the track, Emily pulled out her sketchbook and drew a picture of the engine, with thick, curly smoke surrounding it.

"That's a good picture," said Edward peeking over her shoulder. "I wish we'd ridden inside that train instead of being battered on top of that flatcar."

The train slowed down and stopped. The children watched as one by one the dignitaries stepped off. The men all wore long dark coats and tall top hats.

"I wonder which one is Sanford Fleming," said Edward. "I'm going to ask someone."

Matt and Emily watched Edward march over to a man with a wide white beard wearing a top hat.

"Excuse me, sir," Edward said. "But could you tell me where I might find Sanford Fleming?"

The man in the top hat laughed. "Right here, young man. What can I do for you?"

"You're Sanford Fleming!" said Edward. "I'm glad to meet you, sir. I've heard about your amazing surveying work. Do you know my friend, Alex Smith?"

"Alex Smith. Of course," said Sanford

Fleming. "Fine young man. I heard he was hurt in an accident recently."

"He's not dead, is he?" asked Edward.

"I hope not, although I understand his injuries were severe."

"Do you know where I can find him?" asked Edward.

"No. I've been away from this area for a while. But come see me after the ceremony, and I'll ask some men who might know."

"Thank you, sir," said Edward shaking Mr. Fleming's hand.

"Don't thank me yet," said Sanford Fleming. "Why don't you and your friends walk to the ceremony with me? What are your names?"

"I'm Edward."

"I'm Matt."

"I'm Emily."

Sanford Fleming raised his eyebrows.

"A girl?" he said. "Does your family know you're here, young lady? They must be worried about you."

"I'm sure they're not worried," said Emily.

"Well, they should be. This is no place for a young girl. It's rough and dangerous. Be careful, Emily."

8

Do It Again

A crowd was gathering near the rails. The men in the long coats and tall hats stood in front.

"Come on," said Edward. "I want a front row view. I don't want to miss a thing."

Edward hurried ahead and wiggled his way into the crowd. Soon he was standing in the front row beside all the railroad officials.

"Do you want to sneak in front, too?" Matt asked Emily.

"No. I can see from here if I stand on my tiptoes."

"Me too. And I'm turning my recorder on to get the sound of the last spike being driven into the rails. It's too crowded over there. No one will see me here." Matt slipped the recorder out of his pocket and held it under his jacket.

They watched the railroad workers drive in spike after spike. Then it was time for the last spike. Everyone waited to see who would get the honour of pounding it in. A white-bearded man in a top hat stepped forward.

"Mr. Donald Smith is going to drive the last spike in!" said a man beside them.

"It's not surprising," said a tall man. "He paid for a lot of the railroad."

Donald Smith lifted the sledgehammer. Everyone watched as it came down, but the spike didn't go into the rail. Mr. Smith missed!

"Oh no!" whispered Emily to Matt. "He bent the spike!"

"And Edward's staring at him as if he can't believe anyone that important could mess up. Look! They're giving Mr. Smith another chance. The road master is handing him a new spike."

"What's a road master?" asked Emily.

"He's in charge of keeping the railroad working."

"Here goes Mr. Smith again," said Emily.

A photographer snapped a picture as Donald Smith lifted the hammer again. Everyone's eyes were glued to him as he aimed.

He banged the hammer down.

This time the spike went in! Mr. Smith did it! He put the hammer down, smiled, and stepped back.

For a minute no one moved or spoke. And then a man cheered. Immediately, the whole crowd exploded into applause and congratulations. Emily and Matt shook hands with all the men around them. The train's whistle blew and the cameraman took more pictures.

The cheering slowly died down and everyone turned to another man in a long, black coat with a dark beard. "Speech!" Speech!" they cried.

"It's Mr. Van Horne!" said the men beside Emily and Matt.

"Why is he making a speech?" asked Emily.

"Because without Van Horne there would be no railroad. He never stopped working for it, no matter how tough things got." said a tall railroad worker.

Mr. Van Horne stepped forward and made a short speech.

"Hurrah! Bravo! We did it!" The crowd burst into more excited talk and applause.

Suddenly men rushed around, grabbing bits of rail, bits of the broken spikes, handfuls of dirt, bits of anything they could find.

"Everyone wants a souvenir," said Matt, laughing.

"Look, what I found," said Edward. "I wonder who dropped this?"

It was a train whistle, just like the one Emily and Matt had found in the dresser! "I'm going to keep it forever," said Edward.

Emily winked at Matt. They both knew that the whistle had brought them to see the Last Spike.

9

Don't Give Up

"All aboard for the Pacific!" the train conductor called.

The railroad officials headed for the train.

"Oh no," said Edward. "They're all going. I have to talk to Mr. Fleming about Alex. Where is he?"

"There!" said Matt, pointing toward a small group of men near the train.

The children raced over to Sanford Fleming.

"I was just about to look for you," he told

them. "I'm afraid I have to leave. But I asked some people about Alex. Unfortunately, no one's seen him for a while. I'm sorry I don't have any more news."

Edward swallowed hard. "Thank you, sir," he said. He turned and walked away.

"Hey, wait up!" said Matt. He ran after Edward.

"Poor boy," said Sanford Fleming to Emily. "I wish I could help him."

The train whistle blew again. "All aboard!" called the conductor louder.

"Goodbye, Mr. Fleming," said Emily. She turned to join Edward and Matt.

"Wait," said Sanford Fleming.

Emily spun around.

Sanford Fleming reached into his coat pocket. "Here. Give this to Edward to help Alex. I hope he finds him, and I hope Alex will recover from his injuries." Mr. Fleming handed Emily a sack of coins.

Emily stared at the money. She didn't know what to do.

"Take it, please. It's the least I can do. So many men have given their lives to build this railroad. I hope Alex Smith isn't one of them."

"Wow! Thanks," said Emily, shaking Mr. Fleming's hand.

Sanford Fleming smiled. Then with a tip of his hat, he bid Emily goodbye and bounded up the train steps.

Emily raced over to Edward and Matt. "Look," she said. "Mr. Fleming gave you this money to help Alex."

Edward's eyes widened as Emily opened the sack full of coins.

"Wait here," said Edward. He ran toward the train.

The train was belching black smoke and beginning to move.

"Mr. Fleming! Mr. Fleming!" Edward shouted, running alongside the train.

Just as the train picked up speed, Sanford Fleming appeared at one of the windows. He slid the window open and poked his head out.

"Good luck, Edward!" he called, waving. "Don't give up. You'll find Alex. I'm sure of it."

"Thank you, sir. Thank you for everything!"

Edward watched the train chug down the tracks. Then he ran back to Emily and Matt.

"I'm glad I have some money, but where do I look for Alex now? No one knows where he is. It's like he's disappeared...or maybe..." Tears sprang into Edward's eyes. He brushed them away. "He can't be gone. I have to find him. But how?"

10

Stinky as Socks

"Look down there!" said Matt, pointing to an area near the tracks. "There are tents and rundown shacks. That must be where the railroad workers live."

"Maybe they know about Alex," said Emily.

"Let's go down there and see what we can find out. It's worth a try," said Edward.

Emily, Matt, and Edward hurried toward a small ramshackle hut. The path was strewn with broken rail spikes, split railway ties, tree stumps, and rocks.

"Anybody home?" Edward called when they neared the hut.

No one answered.

"There's a funny smell around here," said Matt.

"It's the smell of tobacco, beer, sweat, cedar, and straw," explained Edward. "It's the smell around railroad camps. You get used to it."

"I don't think I'd ever get used to it," said Emily, holding her nose. "It's stinky. It's worse than dirty socks."

"You don't notice the smell after a while," said Edward. He poked his head into the hut. "No one's in here."

"Let's see if anyone's in the tents," suggested Emily.

They walked over to a tent.

"Anyone home?" Edward called.

No one answered there.

They walked to the next tent. No one was there either. They checked two more tents. They were all smelly but empty. They checked out a large empty shack. "Someone was cooking beans here awhile ago, but they took their cooking supplies. What's going on?"

"Maybe they're having a meeting somewhere else," said Matt.

"Why would they have a meeting, and where would they go?" asked Edward, looking around.

"Let's check things out that way," said Matt pointing to the left.

The group walked beside the newly laid tracks. They looked everywhere for railroad workers, but they didn't see a single person.

The wind blew. It was chilly and damp. Emily pulled her jacket tightly around her. "What are we going to do now?" she asked.

"What if everyone's left?"

"The train will return—sometime, although I don't know when," said Edward. "And we can always walk. I've walked for days when I've had no choice."

"I don't want to walk for days," groaned Emily.

"Wait!" said Matt. "I smell something. It's food! Someone's cooking!"

"Hurray! There are people over there," said Emily. She pointed to a spot in the distance, where a group of men were gathered.

The children charged over. A bunch of railway workers were sitting on rocks and tree stumps beside the tracks. Some were cooking. Others were talking and sipping steaming cups of coffee.

A tall, broad-shouldered man with a large droopy mustache beckoned to them. "Come join us!" he called. "We're having our own Last Spike celebration."

"Thanks!" said Emily and Matt.

"Do you know a railroad worker named Alex Smith?" asked Edward.

"Yes," said the tall man, who said his name was Tim. "Poor fellow."

"He-he isn't…," stammered Edward.

"Don't worry. Alex is not dead, although he almost died. His buddy Roger took good care of him. Someone said that Alex and Roger might even be coming to join our celebration today."

Edward's face broke into a grin. He jumped up and cheered so loudly that everyone laughed. Then he shook hands with all the men. "That's the best news I've ever heard!"

11

Watch Out!

"Look! There's Alex and Roger now! I never thought I'd see Alex walk again, but he is!"

Tim pointed to two men heading toward them. The shorter of the men was about eighteen and leaning on a stick. He brushed his curly black hair out of his eyes as he stopped to rest every few minutes. His face looked drawn and tired.

"Alex!" called Edward. He raced toward his friend. "Alex. It's me. Edward!"

The man with the stick looked up.

A big smile creased the man's weary face. "Edward! I can't believe you're here!"

Emily and Matt watched Edward embrace Alex and shake hands with Roger. They heard Edward thank Roger for helping Alex. But before Edward could say anything else, they could hear a loud rumbling.

"What's that?" asked Emily.

"Up there!" said Matt, pointing up the hillside. "Rocks!"

A pile of rocks was careening down the hill, heading right for Edward, Alex, and Roger.

"Watch out!" yelled Emily.

"Rock slide!" called Matt. "Get out of the way!"

Edward looked up. He grabbed Alex and pulled him away from the rock slide. But Roger didn't have time to jump out of the way. A large rock hit his leg.

Roger fell to the ground, clutching his leg and moaning.

Alex and Edward bent over him.

"Can you walk?" Alex asked.

Roger nodded his head. "I...I...don't know. My ankle hurts bad."

Edward and Alex glanced up the hill behind them. Rocks hung on the edge. They looked like they were about to tumble down to the ground, too.

"Quick! We need to get out of here!" said Alex.

"Wait here!" said Edward. He ran toward Emily and Matt, but Emily and Matt were already hurrying toward him. Matt was carrying the sled in his arms.

"You read my mind," said Edward.

"We want to help," said Emily.

Matt put the sled down beside Roger.

Matt and Edward helped Roger stand up and sit on the sled.

"I'll pull," said Edward.

Edward pulled Roger along the muddy and bumpy path as quickly as he could. Alex and Emily followed.

They were almost back with the rest of the railroad workers when there was another rumble, louder than before. In an instant, rocks crashed down to the spot where they'd just stood.

"Phew. That was close," said Edward. He stared at the pile of rocks on the ground. "We would have been crushed by those rocks, for sure. Thank goodness for your sled."

"Thanks," said Alex to Emily and Matt. Then he turned to Roger. "How's your ankle?"

"It hurts, but I don't think it's broken. If you help me, I think I can even stand."

Roger winced and bit his lip as two railroad workers ran over to help him up. Roger's legs wobbled, but he took a few steps holding onto the men.

"Why don't you lie down in my tent?" Tim offered. "We'll help you walk back."

"Let's all head back," said another railroad worker. "Tomorrow we'll be working again. We could all use some sleep."

"Edward, you and the children can bunk down with me. It may be a bit crowded, but it's all we have," said Tim.

Emily glanced at Matt. She knew he was thinking the same thing she was. There's no way she wanted to sleep in that dirty, smelly tent. She didn't even want to step inside the tent. But how could she say that to Tim? He was trying to help them.

"I'm not sleepy," said Emily.

"Me neither," said Matt.

"Suit yourselves, children," said Tim. "But the tent is more comfortable than the ground."

Matt glanced at Emily. Tim was right, but neither of them wanted to sleep on the ground or in the tent. But what could they do?

Matt picked up the sled. As he did, he glanced at the front of the sled. Shimmery gold words were forming.

You rode the rails.
You helped today.
But now you must
Be on your way.

Matt tapped Emily on the shoulder.

"Em," he whispered. "Look at the sled. It's time to go home."

Emily glanced at the front of the sled and nodded. "We have to tell everyone that we need to stay behind."

"How?" asked Matt.

"I know."

Emily stopped walking. "I have to tie my shoelaces," she announced to the railway workers.

"We'll catch up with you soon," said Matt.

"Well, don't hang around here by yourself for long," said Tim. "There are bears around."

"We know," said Matt. "We saw some."

"You're lucky they didn't come after you. Come on, everybody. Let's go."

Emily and Matt waved as Tim, Edward, Alex, Roger, and the railway workers headed down the tracks.

"Quick. Behind that tree so they don't see us fly," said Matt to Emily.

"I bet their eyes would pop right out of their heads if they did," said Emily laughing.

Emily and Matt dragged the sled behind a large tree.

"Wait! We didn't say goodbye," said Emily. She ripped out her picture of the train from her sketchbook. She wrote: *We're fine. Don't worry. Matt and Emily.* Then she left the picture on a tree stump and put a rock on it to keep it in place.

"It might blow away from there or get drenched in the rain or snow," said Matt.

"So where should I leave it?"

"How about in here," suggested Matt. He picked up a hat. "Edward dropped his hat. I'll bet he will come back for this as soon as he realizes he dropped it. If you put your picture and note deep inside, he's sure to find it. And it will stay dry inside."

"Good idea!" Emily placed her picture deep inside Edward's hat and left it on the tree stump.

"Now let's fly!" She hopped on the sled beside Matt.

As soon as Emily sat down, the sled rose.

The sled flew over the tracks, over the trees, over the mountains, and into a fluffy white cloud.

They were back in Emily's tower.

"Amazing! There's not a drop of mud on the sled or on my shoes. We left all the muck behind," said Emily.

"It was great finally seeing an old train," said Matt. "I just wish I could have had a ride in it instead of on that dirty flatcar."

"I wish we'd eaten some tasty food, like railroad pie."

"What's that?" asked Matt.

"Apples, honey, stale bread, and a sprinkling of broken railroad spikes. I hear it's *dee-licious*."

Matt laughed. "Emily! That's crazy!"

Emily smiled. "I know but there's some real apple pie in the fridge that really *is* delicious! Follow me to the kitchen, Matt. I don't know about you, but I'm as hungry as a bear!"

MORE ABOUT...

After their adventure, Matt and Emily wanted to know more about the railroad and bears. Turn the page for their favourite facts.

Matt's Top Ten Facts

1. The railroad workers held their own "unoffical" Last Spike ceremony. There's a famous photo of it.

2. In 1881, Major A. B. Rogers discovered the pass through the Selkirk Mountains—the only way to go by rail from East to West.

> We saw him at the Last Spike ceremony! -E.

3. The train that brought the dignitaries who attended the Last Spike ceremony had a polished brass boiler and a diamond-shaped smokestack.

4. In 1885, Edward Mallandaine's work transporting road-building supplies had dried up. He was on his way home to Victoria, British Columbia, when he hopped a freight train to see the Last Spike ceremony.

5. After the ceremony, Edward worked in Victoria as an architect and engineer. Later, he fought in World War One.

6. A silver spike had been made for the Last Spike ceremony, but they used a plain iron spike instead.

7. Donald Smith kept the bent spike as a souvenir. He had bits of it shaved off and set with diamonds for his wife and the wives of other dignitaries.

> Did they wear them like earrings? Pretty spiky! -E.

8. On the day of the Last Spike ceremony, a terrible Canadian Pacific company accident occurred: a CP steamer, the *Algoma*, sank in Ontario, killing 45 people.

9. Although November 7, 1885, was the day celebrated for linking the railroad from east to west, there were still parts of the railroad to finish before trains could regularly cross Canada.

10. The promise that the railroad would be completed was one of the reasons that British Columbia agreed to become part of Canada.

Emily's Top Ten Facts

1. In 1862, Sanford Fleming, the famous surveyor of the railroad, suggested a railroad be built all the way to the Pacific. It was built 23 years later.

2. It was hard to build the railroad. People often worked from early morning to late at night.

3. They caused rockslides and avalanches when they used dynamite to blast through rock and trees.

5. Building the railroad was dangerous work. Some men were injured and even killed.

4. Railroad workers lived in tents, boxcars, log or mud huts, and shanties made from wood planks. These places smelled of tobacco, steaming wood, and people who hardly ever took a bath.

Yeah! We saw them. We smelled them!
—M.

6. Some of the men who built the railroad weren't prepared for how tough it was going to be. They'd taken the job because they'd needed the money.

7. The Last Spike was a simple ceremony because the Canadian Pacific Railroad couldn't afford a big, fancy party. They'd used up their money building the railroad.

8. Black bears usually stay in their dens from November until April, but sometimes they come out to stretch and hunt for food.

9. February and March are the only months when black bears sleep so soundly that they stay in their dens the whole time.

When it's really cold in February, I wish I could sleep the whole month! —M.

10. Black bears usually avoid humans, but if they want food, they'll topple garbage cans, knock over birdfeeders, and even try to enter buildings.

So You Want to Know...
FROM AUTHOR FRIEDA WISHINSKY

When I was writing this book, my friends wanted to know more about the Chinese workers who contributed so much to building the railroad. I told my friends that *All Aboard!* was based on historical facts; Edward Mallandaine, Sanford Fleming, and Donald Smith were all real people. Although the Chinese workers were also real people, few can be identified by name. And their story was not a happy one. Here are some questions I answered:

Why were Chinese workers invited to come to British Columbia to work on the railroad?

The railroad had to be constructed through mountainous land in British Columbia. The work was difficult and dangerous, and local workers were in short supply. So Chinese labourers were invited to build this treacherous portion of the railroad.

Between 1881 and 1884, about 17,000 Chinese men came to B.C. to build the railroad.

Why did the Chinese workers decide to travel all the way from China to work on the railroad?

Between 1852 and 1908, China suffered 14 floods, 7 typhoons, 4 earthquakes, 2 droughts, 14 plagues, and 5 famines. These natural disasters contributed to political unrest. There was also not enough land to farm and a growing population to feed. With all these problems, many Chinese workers were desperate for a job. When the opportunity came to build the railroad, they grabbed it.

What were the pay and working conditions like for the Chinese railroad workers?

The Chinese workers earned $1.00 a day and still had to pay for their own food and housing. White workers were paid $1.50–$2.00 a day, and they didn't have to pay for their own food and lodging. The Chinese workers were also given the most dangerous work. They had to clear the railway's roadbed by blasting through rock. Accidents and fires were common and little medical help was available when a worker was injured.

How did the Chinese workers live?

The workers lived in camps, sleeping tents, or boxcars. They cooked on open outdoor fires. Their diet consisted mainly of rice, dried salmon, and tea. They didn't make enough money to buy fresh fruit and vegetables, so many of the workers came down with an illness called scurvy, a disease that hits people who lack vitamin C in their diet.

Why did some of the other residents of British Columbia resent the Chinese workers and discriminate against them?

Some people were afraid that the Chinese would take their jobs away. Andrew Onderdonk, an engineer who was given the contract to build part of the railroad, said he'd only hire Chinese workers if he couldn't find others to do the job. When he couldn't find reliable people, he hired Chinese labourers from the United States. When he needed more men, he hired workers from China.

What happened to the Chinese workers when the railroad was completed?

When the job was finished, the labourers were let go. Some found work back in China. Others found work in other British Columbia industries like forestry, fishing, coal mining, and domestic service. After 1885, new Chinese immigrants were charged a "head tax" to enter Canada. That tax, and others the Chinese were forced to pay over the next years, cut down on Chinese immigration to Canada.

Coming next in the
Canadian Flyer Adventures Series...

Canadian Flyer Adventures
#10

Lost in
the Snow

Emily and Matt visit New France where a
blizzard threatens the safety of their new friend.

Visit
www.mapletreepress.com/canadianflyeradventures
for a sneak peek at the latest book in the series.

The *Canadian Flyer*
Adventures Series

#1 Beware, Pirates!   **#2 Danger, Dinosaurs!**   **#3 Crazy for Gold**

#4 Yikes, Vikings!   **#5 Flying High!**   **#6 Pioneer Kids**

#7 Hurry, Freedom   **#8 A Whale Tale**   **#9 All Aboard!**

Upcoming Book

Look out for the next book that will take
Emily and Matt on a new adventure:

#10 Lost in the Snow

And more to come!

More Praise for the Series

"[Emily and Matt] learn more than they ever could have from a history textbook. Every book in this new series promises to shed light on a different chapter of Canadian history."
~ *MONTREAL GAZETTE*

"Readers are in for a great adventure."
~ *EDMONTON'S CHILD*

"This series makes Canadian history fun, exciting and accessible."
~ *CHRONICLE HERALD (HALIFAX)*

"[An] enthralling series for junior-school readers."
~ *HAMILTON SPECTATOR*

"...highly entertaining, very educational but not too challenging. A terrific new series."
~ *RESOURCE LINKS*

"This wonderful new Canadian historical adventure series combines magic and history to whisk young readers away on adventure...A fun way to learn about Canada's past."
~ *BC PARENT*

"Highly recommended."
~ *CM: CANADIAN REVIEW OF MATERIALS*

Teacher Resource Guides now available online.
Please visit our website at
www.mapletreepress.com/canadianflyeradventures
to download tips and ideas for
using the series in the classroom.

About the Author

Frieda Wishinsky, a former teacher, is an award-winning picture- and chapter-book author, who has written many beloved and bestselling books for children. Frieda enjoys using humour and history in her work, while exploring new ways to tell a story. Her books have earned much critical praise, including a nomination for a Governor General's Award in 1999. In addition to the books in the *Canadian Flyer Adventures* series, Frieda has published *What's the Matter with Albert?*, *A Quest in Time*, and *Manya's Dream* with Maple Tree Press. Frieda lives in Toronto.

About the Illustrator

Leanne Franson has drawn as long as she can remember, and even before! She drew in her school notebooks, on scrap paper, on the sidewalk. And she read and read, especially stories that took place in the past, or had children who travelled to other and distant worlds. Leanne has lent her pencil and brush to over 80 books, and is happy to be accompanying Matt and Emily back into history in the *Canadian Flyer Adventures* series. Leanne works at home in Montreal, where she lives with her son Benjamin Taotao, her Saint Bernard, Gretchen, and two cats.